Isaac Bassett Choate

Obeyd, the Camel Driver

Isaac Bassett Choate

Obeyd, the Camel Driver

ISBN/EAN: 9783744790154

Printed in Europe, USA, Canada, Australia, Japan

Cover: Foto ©Andreas Hilbeck / pixelio.de

More available books at **www.hansebooks.com**

OBEYD, THE CAMEL DRIVER

BY

ISAAC BASSETT CHOATE

*The camel driver has his thoughts, and the
camel — he has his thoughts*
—Arabic Proverb

NEW YORK
HOME JOURNAL PRINT
1899

To her the beaming of whose tender eyes
Tells what beyond the power of language lies,
    Whose dear companionship through desert place
Of all the desert makes a paradise.

CONTENTS

THE CAMEL DRIVER'S THOUGHTS

WHAT gems and pearls by camel train are brought,
Sweet breath of roses, mantles richly wrought!
   For those who loiter in life's market-place
The driver brings companionable thought.

THE CAMEL DRIVER'S THOUGHTS

I

I cross the desert as men cross the sea,
A long, lone journey traveled silently;
 With nothing beautiful the heart to cheer
But thoughts of Allah,—Allah's thought of me.

II

Two friends stand talking in the city gates,
One goes abroad, at home the other waits;
 To which the better fortune, who can tell?
In wiser hand than ours lie human fates.

III

The time is come the last farewell to say,
With prayers must friend speed friend upon his way;
 We're parting now, and none but Allah knows
If this our present parting be for aye.

IV

A sad leave-taking at the parting well,—
One braves the desert's dangers weird and fell
    Back turns the other to a lonely home,
And Allah goes with both,—how strange to tell!

V

This march across the desert waste begun,
The stars will guide by night, by day the sun;
    But backward o'er that track both day and night
To home and friends will Thought unerring run.

VI

Love joins us with so fair a tale to tell
We travel with him under magic spell,
    Nor think to ask our dear companion's name
Before he turns aside and says, "Farewell!"

VII

Since of our earthly lot is nothing sure
Except that earthly joys may not endure,
    At every stage what better course to take
Than try to make our present joy secure?

VIII

Not to enjoy the vain and fugitive,
To taste fair fruits the smiling seasons give,
But griefs and losses bravely to endure,
This is to live and deeply feel we live.

IX

These camels, forced their heavy loads to bear,
O'er native sands by paths familiar fare;
But he who drives, a stranger and alone,
Himself by Fate is driven he knows not where.

X

Worn desert paths, in sandy furrows seen,
From gardens lead to other gardens green,
As human lives lead out from regions blest
To others blest,—but oh, the dust between!

XI

From morning's calm to quietude of eve
Slow moving camels dusty courses weave,—
From birth to death we fret life's dusty plain,
And at our death how little dust we leave!

XII

Trails cross but once however long they be,
As ship hails ship but once upon the sea,
 Let then there be fair greeting and God-speed
Between each passing traveler and me.

XIII

We needs must part, we who have strangely met
Halfway between where rise the stars and set;
 We needs must part, athwart our courses run,
We'll say good-bye and nevermore forget.

XIV

The paths we take this way and that divide,
We follow them till as the desert wide;
 And yet, perchance, these paths may join again,
And we be comrades on the further side.

XV

Eternity is long and Allah can
At leisure form and execute His plan,
 But time is short, — the time wherein to learn
To do one's duty to his fellow-man.

XVI

As sailors watch the stars upon the sea
So on our desert stages travel we,
    Not knowing that, whatever course we take,
Along that selfsame path comes Destiny.

XVII

" This, too, will pass," the Persian proverb saith,
This weal or woe, as goes the zephyr's breath;
    Be fortune good or ill. it travels past—
Not so goes past inevitable Death.

XVIII

Love draws for us the line of duty straight
Across the sands of life to further gate,
    Love goes the way to guide our erring steps
To where for us do patient angels wait.

XIX

The sun at night goes to his tent of red,
With darkness is the desert overspread;
    So deeply dark the curtain that is drawn
At last between the living and the dead.

XX

Within the empty silence of the night
When all except the heavens is shut from sight,
   Then may we hear the singing of the stars—
A music shed from their celestial height.

XXI

How Hope's fair promise round about us lies
As far horizon bounds the earth and skies,
   And as that line moves on with our advance
So, while we follow, Hope before us flies.

XXII

With cries of men are daily stages passed,
We tent at night in silence deep and vast;
   With noisy striving we push on through life,
The tranquil cypress shelters us at last.

XXIII

Through evening's falling shade do stars grow bright,
And desert skies hang lower in the night;
   Amid the doubt and gloom of troubled days
Fair peace of Heaven shows nearer mortal sight.

XXIV

Bright shining stars remain unseen by day,
Night makes them visible by softest ray;
  And so it is the smiling of a friend
The brighter shines seen on the darker way.

XXV

As stars upon celestial pastures are
Steadfast and fixed, each by its neighbor star,
  So on the sand the moving caravan
Seems motionless, watched by us from afar.

XXVI

Fair Shiraz boasts that Allah's gifts are shed
On her, few glories o'er the desert spread;
  Why need more stars be shown us in the night
While countless are those shining overhead?

XXVII

When I behold day's monarch set or rise,
Reflect what glory then around me lies,
  And try to feign what heaven is like, I think
That desert is some part of Paradise.

XXVIII

With wings of flame do clouds of evening sweep
Across the sky as ships across the deep;
   Within that glow of sunset angels stand
To guard the world below them, fast asleep.

XXIX

We dream of music in the silent night,
We dream of beauty where there is no light;
   To those who rest within the tent of green
These dreams are real to hearing and to sight.

XXX

Were we all hours of life with sunlight blessed,
Did never sun go down behind the west,
   How many other worlds were never known!
How many suns besides were never guessed!

XXXI

O realm of peace, where light and glory meet!
O realm of beauty, glad with angel feet!
   Ye clouds above the desert's darkening plain,
Whereon hath Allah placed his Mercy Seat!

XXXII

In her own shadow Night goes by, and then
Comes genial light of day to waking men;
    But since the dead wake not from their long sleep
For them the day will never break again.

XXXIII

In search of Allah men unhappy stray
On arid wastes of thought day after day,
    To find, alas! o'erwearied with their toil,
They left him when they started on their way.

XXXIV

In market-place, in city gates one hears
Opinions variable as hopes and fears,
    From youth to age do moods of people change,
But Truth is changeless through revolving years.

XXXV

By day around us ambient light is shed,
By night do faithful stars watch overhead,
    The heavens remain unchanged throughout the years,
While earth slips from us as its paths we tread.

XXXV

We fold our tents soon as the day's begun,
We pitch our tents soon as the day is done;
   The same horizon girdling all around
Shows us how nearly birth and death are one.

XXXVII

The rising and the setting stars are dim,
Seem farthest off, seen near the desert's rim;
   Deep awe of Allah wakens in the soul
With wakening thought that 'tis a part of Him.

XXXVIII

Look at the stars—how steadily they keep
Appointed way while heaven's blue vault they sweep!
   See then how man goes stumbling in the dark—
For such a life as this should mortals weep?

XXXIX

Man's spirit, offspring of the Over-soul,
Flies to its source as runner to the goal
   But all the dead bring no access of gain,—
The parts can add no greatness to the whole.

XL

We judge of distances by shade and light,
Correct by day uncertain guess at night;
   Who says that he stands near by Allah's side
Has failed to judge supernal glories right.

XLI

I cannot answer Where is wisdom found?
Nor where unfailing joys of life abound?
   But faithful camels lead me to the spot
Where running waters slake the parchèd ground.

XLII

Where in the burning sand deep waters spring
Bloom oleanders, happy sparrows sing;
   So when the deepest feelings flood the soul
Diviner thoughts those hidden currents bring.

XLIII

A well of water in the thirsty ground
And groups of waving palm trees stand around;
   Let hope but spring afresh in desert lives
And all the world a paradise is found.

XLIV

Alone we journey on, day after day,
My camel and myself, a lonely way,
   Where even Echo shrinks to set her foot
Or let her lips repeat the words I say.

XLV

A sea of desert sand about me spread,
All life of beast, of bird, of insect, fled,
   I deem myself alone, but Afrit form
Warns me not even desert sand is dead.

XLVI

The world of sense fits well the world of mind,
Man shares a wider life than of mankind,
   From desert's empty floor we gather truth
More than in city's crowded street we find.

XLVII

Poor thorny shrub half-starved in desert spot
Gains there a sweetness garden rose hath not,
   From desert bitterness of lonely life
The soul distils sweet frankincense of thought.

XLVIII

What shouts of joy where Victory folds her wings,
Where host triumphant grateful pæan sings!
    But oh! the bitterness of mute despair
'Mid broken ranks of poor heart-broken things!

XLIX

To him who boldly takes the battlefield
Heaven will extend its all-protecting shield,
    And if he enter service of the Right
For him are books of Fate once more unsealed.

L

A friend we beg that Allah will bestow,
Some fortune, too, that we good-will may show;
    But, if to envious Fate this seem too much,
All but the friend we'll cheerfully forego.

LI

Few friends suffice us while the way is won,
We pitch our tents alone the day is done;
    But sad were coming to the end of life
And finding there the lack of even one.

LII

However short or long the journey made,
My camel halts beneath each friendly shade;
    Along its dusty way let mortal life
At every hour of gladness be delayed.

LIII

Six days for toiling in the field or mart.
Six days for travel and laborious art,
    The seventh, a halting on life's desert road,
Our fathers called "the Resting of the Heart."

LIV

Rose bushes pass the winter stripped and bare,
With spring's green dress white roses gaily wear;
    Why cannot we as patiently await
Our coming joys, nor yield to dark despair?

LV

How blest the happy man who wisely knows
To use such gifts as Allah's hand bestows,
    And what that hand may prudently withhold
Without one least repining thought foregoes!

LVI

Beneath a flaming sun day after day,
Beneath the moon at night we make our way;
   Were in our path a glowworm to appear,
The glowworm were more marvelous than they.

LVII

The false mirage, with show of waters cool,
Turns thirsty desert spot to seeming pool,
   Thus Fortune spreads a vain alluring show
To cheat the fancy of unthinking fool

LVIII

The gifts of fickle Fortune quickly bring
Such empty praise as flattering poets sing,
   The man that wisely rules his heart's desires
Is by the suffrage of mankind their king.

LIX

Blame Fortune not for life's depleted store,
She takes not save what she had given before;
   Count gains and losses you shall surely find
Though much she takes away she gives yet more.

LX

While solid rock is shattered by a blow
In safety lie smooth polished sands below,—
    Proud sovereign Khaliff trembles for his throne,
Not any fear poor camel drivers know.

LXI

Oh, why should Allah have so much regard
For man, and deem his loss of Eden hard!
    Go into exile with Humanity,
Do all for love, do nothing for reward!

LXII

Across the burning sand with padded tread
My patient camel shambles on ahead,
    That track together with my sandalled steps
Will with to-morrow's dust be overspread.

LXIII

On desert sand where fierce the sunbeams burn,
From moving shade our destiny we learn;
    "I come and go," the sun says, "every day,
But when goes man 'tis never to return."

LXIV

Upon the desert's distant, sloping rim
An empty city rises, vast but dim;
   The city of the dead;—one thither fares
A cheerful way, doth Allah go with him!

LXV

Men tell of ghostly trains by phantoms led
That make the desert way with noiseless tread,
   At night these bring from Islam's farthest bounds
To Mecca's holier soil the Moslem dead.

LXVI

"Now have we seen the pageantry of earth,
Its pomp of sorrow and its mime of mirth!"
   My soul exclaims, nor yet observes the while
The grim, gaunt figure crouching at our hearth.

LXVII

Should'st thou, my Soul, with tears and prayers implore
Beyond thy doom one day of life the more,
   Those prayers and weeping would be all in vain;
Unpitying keeper has thy days in store.

LXVIII

How oft before their mortal dwelling stand
Dear Life and Soul together, hand in hand;
    Watch flight of angel on his glad return,
With exile longings for their native land!

LXIX

Were all bright things within our world to know
The overshadowing cloud of human woe,
    Would not that knowledge some fair brightness dim,
And all our world be made the darker so?

LXX

One selfsame path all enter on at birth,
With equal pace advance to shame or worth,—
    In crash of battle, with lone pestilence,
Death's herald cries his empire through the earth.

LXXI

Proud waving fronds the palm lifts to the skies,
The storm is o'er, a log the palm tree lies,—
    Proud rich man dreams of greater fortune yet,
And in that feverish dream of his he dies.

LXXII

The lives of men are cheap where heroes die,
So many offer theirs, so few to buy;
    But let one ask the price on fields of peace
And he will find that lives are rated high.

LXXIII

Bloodhounds of war, strong-jawed, know not release,
Loud-clattering mills of war will never cease;
    The shepherd never pasture flocks of sheep
Nor pitch his tent upon the skirts of Peace.

LXXIV

To leave all that is worth the living for,
To come back to the cypress-shaded or
    To find in foreign land a nameless grave,
This is the fortune joined with glorious war.

LXXV

The victors in the fight a captive hold,
They offer him his life for sum of gold;
    The balance of that life he cannot know,
The price of ransom easily is told.

LXXVI

Upon the battlefield the victor saith,
" To you is life given back for change of faith ; "
   In bargain of so simple terms it seems
The honest, free man's choice were surely death.

LXXVII

My longing climbs the steep and rugged way
Where riders spur their horses to the fray ;
   A helpless prisoner of Fate am I —
The heart's beloved is fairest when away !

LXXVIII

Snow on the mountain, on the thirsty plain
Is soft and cooling touch of gentle rain ;
   We 've disappointment to weigh down our pride,
Sweet ministries of love to soothe our pain.

LXXIX

One fancies what we commonly behold,
Another fancies what is quaint or old ;
   If there were not diversity of taste
The potter's ugly jar were never sold.

LXXX

A gem in golden setting richly wrought
May with the ransom of a king be bought,
   But if my taste mislike the showy thing
The showy thing is rightly valued nought.

LXXXI

The glow of wine, the savor of rich food,
The sheen of silk, the grace of womanhood,
   The pomp of wealth, unmeaning shouts of fame,
To worldly-minded these are all their good.

LXXXII

Where comes a soul all radiant and fair,
Its veil of purity preserved with care,
   It matters nought—the body's lack of grace,
It matters less what raiment this may wear.

LXXXIII

If, O my soul! we take not up the load
Of loss and labor on life's rugged road,
   In vain all hope that we may ever reach
Those heights on which is Glory's bright abode.

LXXXIV

Youth waits at opening gates of manhood long,
The soul thrilled with high purpose fixed and strong; —
   An interlude of sweetest melody
Between the breaking silence and the song.

LXXXV

With others mourn we loss of wealth, and fain
Would cling to what of fortune may remain,
   With our own soul we mourn the loss of youth
When to the soul that loss is all its gain.

LXXXVI

Who eats content to-day his simple crust
Awaits to-morrow with unshaken trust,
   Believing Allah's mercies manifold
As are the desert's countless grains of dust.

LXXXVII

Be life as narrow as the prison cell.
Be life as broad as lands where Bedouins dwell, —
   Great store or nought, 'tis all the same to Time,
For when Time goes goes all of earth as well.

LXXXVIII

Times come and go by turns, revolving fast,
Nor pain nor pleasure e'er were known to last,
But while our life is as a treasure held
We may not grieve for any pleasure past.

LXXXIX

When, overcome by mystery and dread,
From Allah's presence man has turned and fled,
How has he marveled in his soul to find
That Allah's spirit followed not—but led!

XC

At night the stars move in procession slow
Down to the underworld of Death below;
If long or short the ropes by which they're drawn,
Or whose the hands that draw, we may not know.

XCI

Remote as is yon bright star shining fair
Kind providence of Allah blesses there,
While at my feet in clump of scrubby sage
Does sparrow's brood sleep safe in Allah's care.

XCII

At dawn, 'tis said, swings open Eden's gate,
Its hinge yields willingly at evening late,
  For angels have so many ways to go
They're never asked for long outside to wait.

XCIII

Men often ask, Is there aught good in life?
Some sweet reward for all this toil and strife?
  Yea, answer I, for I have seen its good
When looking on my children and my wife.

XCIV

Come, Soul of loved one, with a joyous bound
Join Soul of mine to stray life's garden round,
  And, looking frankly each in other's eyes,
Confess no greater joy in life is found.

XCV

Small children in our homes—what else are they
But our hearts walking with us on our way?
  Let but the breeze blow on them and our eyes
All night to Slumber's wooing answer, "Nay."

XCVI

A child that calls out, "Mother!" in its fears,
Whose feeble cry no more the mother hears,
    Stirs in the father's heart a living fount
That fills his sleepless eyes brimful of tears.

XCVII

O thou, one half my soul, in yonder skies!
How mourns the other half where Hosein lies!
    Athirst for sweet companionship of yore
Though floods of tears fall from o'erflowing eyes.

XCVIII

To Fancy's view time as a sea appears,
Eternity the depth, as waves the years;
    And every drop of that unfathomed flood
Has been made briny with the salt of tears.

XCIX

How slowly herded stars graze o'er their plain
While soul of mine endures this racking pain!
    To me they seem poor helpless fettered things
Or tethered each with adamantine chain,

C

Day follows night so close their traces blend,
Warmth after winter's cold will Allah send;
   'Tis wise to treat good fortune as a guest,
Nor think that woe will never, never end.

CI

The hours of day are blessed with constant light,
To constant shade are doomed the hours of night;
   Where love shines on the pathway of our lives,
'Neath sun, 'neath cloud, that path is always bright.

CII

Within the tent, beneath its darkened shade,
For weary guest the slumber-place is made;
   The traveler coming late to tent of green,
On waiting couch his toil-worn limbs are laid.

CIII

By pilgrim journeying on desert wide
To dweller in the tent is greeting cried,
   "Fair peace be on thy covering in the morn
When shall the world with light be glorified!"

CIV

We know what Now unfolds to eye and ear,
What brought the Past is held in memory dear,
  Before the knowledge which the Future brings
We stand in mystery shrouded and in fear.

CV

We spend our life's best years in toil and pain,
To solve Life's problem seeking all in vain;
  Would clear the mystery of our being here,
And with that effort weary heart and brain.

CVI

High mountain peaks with snow are silvered o'er,
In shadow-haunted vales dark rivers pour;—
  A man may wear a smile upon his face
And at his heart be sick with anguish sore.

CVII

Who mourns the hero in rebellion slain?
His sword, his spear, his shield with bloody stain,
  And one true friend – the steed that goes to drink
At brink of stagnant pool with trailing rein.

CVIII

By succoring the abject and abhorred
Men win to gracious favor of our Lord,
   Not by prayer-rug worn thin with constant use
Is earned of our poor life its great reward.

CIX

Who gathers friends by helping in their need,
Who shields their honor by a kindly deed,
   Grows mightier than the strength of single hand,
Grows richer than the grasp of selfish greed.

CX

Men make excuse for haste the hope to find
Some fond ideal of the youthful mind,
   Loth to admit their anxious thought is fear
Of fancied evils following close behind.

CXI

The generous youth with noble zeal inspired
Runs life's fair race until his soul is tired,
   And thinks him lucky if at last he gain
Some little of all that his heart desired.

CXII

Youth keeps its treasures with a nerveless hold,
Youth counts the hours a tale already told;
    Age, grown more miserly, would be most glad
If but the new-born year brought back the old.

CXIII

The world is burdened with the bitter cry,
We live so little time, so soon we die!
    As justly camel driver might complain,
Too short the desert march, the end too nigh!

CXIV

Here have we through a careless childhood played,
Here later have with idle Fancy strayed;
    More guests are coming,—why then, let us say
Good-bye! before our welcome is out-stayed.

CXV

Who travels o'er a dry and desert place
Looks not to see the violet's gentle face,
    For prudent Nature, having happier thought,
Put violets where they gain and give a grace.

CXVI

'Tis not the good, the honest, brave, and wise
That reach the level of admiring eyes;
    White fleck of foam rides on the billow's crest,
On ocean's floor the pearl we covet lies.

CXVII

In heart of man least thought of others' good
Holds space with thought of vast infinitude,
    But where the thought of God holds not its court
Thought of the poor man's woe will not intrude.

CXVIII

In gentle breath of balm the night air blows
That subtler perfume which the day foregoes,
    To guard their hoards against the stealthy winds
Do flowers at night their treasure-houses close.

CXIX

See how the wild rose blushes to confess
'Mid tame surroundings her own loveliness,—
    Fair thought that blossoms for the artist soul
Gives to that soul what trouble to express!

CXX

Tall beaker, wine-cup, flagon, bowl, and jar,
Of earth or crystal, dear and precious are;
    But what gives chiefest value to them all
The skill of potter's hand may make or mar.

·CXXI

In dim bazaar where goods are bought and sold
Fair rugs of Persian weaving are unrolled,
    Their rainbow dyes, their texture are displayed,
But ne'er is shown poor weaver growing old.

CXXII

Around the earth do Thought and Fancy roam,
As clouds o'er land, o'er sea as flying foam;
    And yet how gladly both come back to thee,
Dear Heart that lovest more to stay at home!

CXXIII

Who lives 'mid garden bloom of thousand dyes
Is wholly charmed by what about him lies,
    Who journeys not afar on desert waste
Can never know how fair are evening skies.

CXXIV

Till now I never dreamed what conld be done
With waste of tawny sand 'neath setting sun;
   Look! how the light and shade together play!
How smiles and frowning o'er the desert run!

CXXV

The farther on my desert way I ride
The longer seems the desert, seems more wide,
   But let me fare as far as go the stars
I cannot move myself from Allah's side.

CXXVI

Decrees of Fate, foreknowledge absolute,
All points of faith about which men dispute,—
   These matter nought, nor views that men maintain,—
For Truth's defence all lips as well were mute.

CXXVII

The tongue is half the man, the other part
That makes of man a unit is the heart;
   This quarries thought and shapes it into words,
The other wields them as one hurls the dart.

CXXVIII

To speak the truth is well although it may
Involve no more than simple 'yea' or 'nay;'
  Yet better is it, knowing truth the while,
To talk of date-stones idly thrown away.

CXXIX

An empty name, as down of thistle light,
Starts round the world its bold ambitious flight;
  Alas! at eve the ever-lengthening shade
But lengthens to be lost at last in night.

CXXX

As two staunch foes, opposing lance and shield,
Meet Youth and Age upon a hostile field;
  Whatever ground advancing Age may win
That ground must Youth, howe'er reluctant, yield.

CXXXI

Life's troubles, in their long succession seen,
Each on its neighbor trouble seem to lean,
  But never yet two gloomy nights went by
Without the going of a day between.

CXXXII

Is life a burden, with these trials cursed?
To taste misfortune we are not the first,
   And having met this we have come to know
Things can but mend when they are at the worst.

CXXXIII

Did Allah heed our prayers to change his plan
He would from human life all evil ban;
   What then? with pain removed what room were left
For thanks to Allah, gratitude to man?

CXXXIV

With toil and care by day are we oppressed,
Night follows day, with night comes gentle rest;
   When we compare what day, what night affords,
Then may we judge if life or death be best.

CXXXV

Sweet violet blooms in beauty to the eye,
Bright Vesper hangs her lamp in western sky; —
   Some gracious duty waits each human life
Be that life on a lowly plane or high.

CXXXVI

However swift or slow the days that pass
In gloom of silent night they end, alas!
    But, after darkest night, is duly poured
Day's shining sand in Time's inverted glass.

CXXXVII

Some sense of dread the deepening twilight brings,
To Night's dark robes a haunting mystery clings;
    How small for us were terror of the night
Were night to us the shade of angels' wings!

CXXXVIII

I dreamed I was a beggar at Heaven's gate,
Outside its portals patiently did wait;
    But not one mite could Charity bestow
For all came penniless—the small, the great.

CXXXIX

Light-hearted let me go with eager mind
When into Allah's care my soul 's resigned,
    Well knowing that, from usurer's thrifty craft,
More than my self I shall hereafter find.

CXL

Rich sandalwood yields of its fragrant store,
The perfume that remains is all the more,—
    With liberal hand the rich dispense their wealth
To find themselves but richer than before.

CXLI

I have my neighbor while at home I stay,
My fellow traveler on the desert way;
    Be I at home or at remotest bounds,
I have my conscience with me night and day.

CXLII

O thou wayfarer, weary Heart of mine,
Sent forth by Allah on some search of thine!
    Let all the dusty road forgotten be
In thinking of thy destiny divine.

CXLIII

Through life we follow paths we do not know,
Close by our side attendant angels go;
    The hand that leads us we remember well
As that which led us years and years ago.

CXLIV

From other worlds that lie beyond the pole
Blow winds that rainless clouds of mystery roll;
   Through life, through death, through time and space
    unchecked,
Deep sighs of Allah sweep across the soul.

CLXV

A hand unseen restrains us and we stay,
Inaudible the voice that warns us, "Nay!"
   And so the camel driver all his life
Conceives he goes a self-directed way.

CXLVI

To camel driver all his earthly pride
Was virtue — opulent in that he died;
   Died poor, men say, for Allah so decreed
That having virtue he have nought beside.

CXLVII

The world itself is governed still by Fate,
Fate rules the subjects and the monarch's state,
   That power obey, submissive to its thrall,
Salute Fate's messenger come soon or late.

CXLVIII

For ills of life man's knowledge has no cure,
And soon or late to all is sorrow sure ;
    Far as Philosophy can lend her aid
She bids mankind be patient and endure.

CXLIX

'Tis only in the tardy autumn late
That sweetness comes unto the ripening date,
    Who labors for the welfare of mankind
For fruit of labor patiently must wait.

CL

Too short for us seem all these toilsome years,
So filled are they with anxious hopes and fears;
    Too short for our, but not for Allah's, plan
Wherein the purpose of our life appears.

CLI

The wood of aloes — ancient proverb saith —
Yields fragrance only to consuming breath,
    Not otherwise the virtues of the good
Embalmed in memories linger after death.

CLII

Twice had the dove gone forth on bootless quest,
Third time she found dry spot on which to rest
    And came not back into the Ark again : —
The dead return not, they have found the best.

CLIII

Before the winter's cold the swallow flies,
Pursues the summer under tropic skies ;
    More kindly impulse to the soul is given
To follow Duty into Paradise.

CLIV

He who would halt before the goal is won,
Would cease from work before the task is done,
    He should reflect day follows after day,
Another morn awaits the setting sun.

CLV

With patience men have toiled so long, so long,
To build the right, to overthrow the wrong !
    Their measured strokes, directed by one thought,
Have blended into harmony of song.

CLVI

For this, man's two-fold gifts were wisely planned,
That feeling heart go with the laboring hand,
　　That while the mortal lives as lives the flower
The spirit learn this life to understand.

CLVII

They 've walked with us and they have shared our fears,
Have bowed with us, with us have mingled tears,—
　　Those lovers of their kind in ages past
As men now walk with men of coming years.

CLVIII

Far off on paths of Paradise are they
Were dear to Allah in life's golden day,
　　The way they went in evening glory lies
Flushed all its length with sunset's level ray.

CLIX

Far must we journey where that pathway lies
In softest light before our longing eyes;
　　Far must we journey, going all alone,
To keep our waited tryst in Paradise.

CLX

Where go the vanished dead at least there's rest
For tired limbs upon our mother's breast,
    And if it be the dead wake not from sleep
We know of Allah's gifts is sleep the best.

CLXI

We are so very weak to Allah's view!
He has no need of me, no need of you,
    And that which makes us precious in His sight
Is what we are, not what our hands can do.

CLXII

Is it the night-breeze whispering in my ear,
Or clamor of Fame's distant voice I hear?
    Perchance an echo from Eternity,
The worlds of sense and spirit are so near!

CLXIII

Strange is the world about us everywhere
Of which our vision tells us it is fair,
    And stranger yet the unseen world as near
Of which we only know the dead are there.

CLXIV

When curious traveler has wandered o'er
The bounds of time he will return no more,
  For when he comes to view eternal scenes
'Gainst his returning angels shut the door.

CLXV

The desert sand is dry the whole night through,
Green blade of grass refreshed by copious dew;
  Let but a friendship spring in human heart
'Tis blessed with tenderness heart never knew.

CLXVI

If we could bar out Sorrow from the heart,
Could from the mind bid gloomy Thought depart,
  Our eyes yet seeing others' deep distress
With brimming tears of tenderness would smart.

CLXVII

All joys of sense with sense must fade away
All joys in truth with truth shall last for aye
  With truth eternal we've eternal home,
A fairer life led in a purer day.

CLXVIII

On many a strand have royal palm trees stood,
Few lands can boast the growth of sandalwood,—
    Amid the throng about the monarch's throne
The great are many, very few the good.

CLXIX

So many a deed of wrong for right is meant,
So many a right one done with ill intent!
    We cannot judge,—then why not kindness give
As on the just and unjust rain is sent?

CLXX

We cannot draw the line through their dense throng,
Tell on which side of this they each belong;
    But this we know, the right makes for the right,
And just as true it is wrong makes for wrong.

CLXXI

Sometimes the lion eager is for fight,
Sometimes the lion safety seeks in flight;
    The warrior need not rush upon the field
Save when he is the champion of Right.

CLXXII

Why should man wish for life a longer day,
Upon its wearying road a longer way;—
　　Full many a flower disdains the Tropic year.
And grows but where keen frosts of winter slay.

CLXXIII

Did virtue in long pilgrimage abide
To Mecca-born were holiness denied,
　　More kind were heaven to those who dwell afar,
More gracious yet had earth been made more wide.

CLXXIV

At home abiding, or on lonely quest,
Heaven in thy bosom bear, to Heaven's behest
　　Bow as a little child, look up to Heaven,
So shall Death find thee fearless and at rest.

CLXXV

Since for mankind death is the common fate,
And when Death calls for us he will not wait;
　　Revenge we gain from good deeds sent before,
Thus Heaven will chide Death that he brings us late.

CLXXVI

Not long may Fortune with one house abide,
Soon comes Adversity with hurried stride,
    Her joy to crush the flower within the bud,
To trample down the weeds of power and pride.

CLXXVII

Keep to the friend who when the times go ill,
When Fortune turns her back, as Fortune will,
    Proves not unfaithful where are others false,
In close companionship rejoices still.

CLXXVIII

What man may court the patronage of Fame
Finds that she speaks inaudibly his name,
    But let one shun her in the market-place
She seeks him out his glory to proclaim.

CLXXIX

How fair are all things bright to childish eyes,
Not less the dark ones when we learn to prize
    Gifts not for their sake but for sake of Him
Whose wisdom grants them and whose love denies.

CLXXX

What is it gilds the sand-heaps and the trees,
That paints the clouds of evening bright as these ?
    What is it but the sunlight's simple ray
Which all uncolored one at noontide sees ?

CLXXXI

This desert sand, a weariness alas !
With pain is watched, seen running in the glass.
    It measures time,—of time we care the more,
Each grain a moment, how the moments pass.

CLXXXII

The sands are quiet when winds cease to blow,
Our spirits calm when passions smoulder low;
    Ah! then we see how vain it was to fret
That Time went as he fancied—fast or slow.

CLXXXIII

All elements, at Nature's stern command,
Against our race in hostile order stand,
    To give earth's glory to the dust again,
Destroy the marvelous triumphs of our hand.

CLXXXIV

A life of toil, a life of penury
This life of mine — I will contented be,
   For this I know, however low its state,
' Tis just the life that Allah meant for me.

CLXXXV

Is it that Death will shut the gates so fast
Which separate the future from this past
   That we, foreknowing here the end of life,
May not discern life's discipline at last ?

CLXXXVI

Day after day with daily march we tire,
  Night after night renew our bivouac fire;
   Thus we grow old, but not the world grows old,—
The world is ever young with young desire.

CLXXXVII

The moods of Fancy are of ample range,
Mirthful, disconsolate ; familiar, strange ;—
   Let desert journey be long as it may
The Desert's temper manifests no change.

CLXXXVIII

Long to the watcher is the weary night
Though patiently he bide the morning light,
    Long is the way to him who seeks for Truth
Though prudently he heed her star aright.

CLXXXIX

The lone wayfarer marks the ways of earth,
Black grief of death, the radiant joy of birth,—
    He marks the joy and grief that come between
To raise immortal souls to nobler worth.

CXC

But though to careless listener standing near
The cries of men discordant may appear,
    Yet when these reach to Allah's throne above
They blend in one appeal to Allah's ear.

CXCI

In regions desolate we tread the dust
Of palaces once cruel with the lust
    Of power and wealth, now sport of idle wind ;—
Ah ! man is impious, and Allah just.

CXCII

Where life is not, Death cannot hold his state,
Where change is not, there is nor soon nor late,—
  ' Tween desert banks the river, dreamless, sleeps,
Bloom lotus buds, and Time forgets his date.

CXCIII

Men say the Sphinx beside the placid Nile
Looks on the desert with as placid smile
  As Fate beholds the destiny of man,
But ne'er relax those stony lips the while.

CXCIV

How have men striven in reason as they could
To learn the source of Evil and of Good;
  Have wearied patient Thought, nor ever dreamed
That Ill is Allah's care—misunderstood.

CXCV

What in this life is but a fond desire
May rise to beauteous action in a higher,—
  How have I seen on bosom of a stream
Fair lotus draw her beauty from the mire !

CXCVI

These desert paths on which we daily wend
A toilsome way but seldom cross or blend,—
    Though wide diverge the separate paths of life
All lead at last but to the selfsame end.

CXCVII

The swallow weaves in air her mystic maze,
The eagle soars beyond our baffled gaze;
    Thus sages, versed in reasoning, rise above
All doubts and fears that cloud life's humble ways.

CXCVIII

How do the songs returning swallows sing
To our glad hearts remembered music bring,
    How sight of flowers with earlier vision blends
Of that fair world where it is always spring !

CXCIX

Not where they meet — the desert and the sky —
On borders mystical to questioning eye
    Expect to find the scenes which Fancy paints, —
As we approach, those prisoning limits fly.

CC

Through all life's changing course of loss and gain
To true believers Hosein's words remain, —
   " If in His care doth Allah shut one gate
In pity and in grace He opens twain."

CCI

Soft falls the rain upon the thirsty sod,
Slight print is left where fleet gazelle has trod, —
   Let but the orphan's tear fall on the ground
Its heavy beat will shake the throne of God.

CCII

With what sweet comradeship of life we fare,
Thou Soul of mine, across the desert bare !
   When at the gates of Heaven thou enterest in
How shall I stand alone and grieving there !

CCIII

Men seem to please themselves with this belief,
With happy days eternity were brief;
   And since this mortal life comes soon to end
Men make life long by filling it with grief.

CCIV

Time makes his course with most unequal pace,
Slowly the past recedes as yielding place,
   The future is outrun by hopes and fears,
The present flies as winner in a race.

CCV

With wearying care and toil is day oppressed,
Night comes and with her cometh gentle rest,
   By day our thoughts outrun the caravan,
With happy dreams our sleep at night is blessed.

CCVI

Day paints the heavens their deep unchanging blue,
Night brings her shining host of stars in view,—
   To one whose life is in the desert spent
Alike are dawn and eve forever new.

CCVII

The wind at night goes past me with a sigh
For fate of man—above, the desert sky
   Seems type of earthly circumstance, and now
Both Night and I are sad—we know not why.

CCVIII

A white sail on the blue unbounded tide,
A white tent pitched upon the desert wide;
   Above them both the same o'erarching heavens,
With both alike doth Allah's care abide.

CCIX

We dream of Paradise as being fair,
A tropic garden bright with flowers rare;
   We wake to realize the pain of life,
Are glad to know its balm is growing there.

CCX

How have I watched the desert through these years!
No dew by night, by day no rain appears,
   No water springs! — to me it seems the Earth
Feels in its heart a grief too deep for tears.

CCXI

To change one primal law is Nature loth,
Living and dead — she is alike to both;
   Fond moth will hover round consuming flame, —
The candle feels no pity for the moth.

CCXII

The hand that gives to man his daily food
Gives just as freely to the raven's brood,
   What gives the gentle dove her harmless ways
Gives to fierce tiger's whelps their thirst for blood.

CCXIII

Outspread beneath our feet the desert lies,
Above our heads unfold the starry skies;
   Why should earth be so dull, the heavens so bright?—
From earth to lift our hearts, to turn our eyes.

CCXIV

The man of wealth who lives in regal state
Must bear with wretched horde about his gate;
   Counsel of sage outvalues merchant's gold,—
How few about the sage's portals wait!

CCXV

Men that have made most praise of worth their own
Are those for whom most spite of men is shown,—
   Were pitcher fashioned from the dust of kings
Some servile hand would break it with a stone.

CCXVI

The potter's wheel runs on with slackening turn.
Beneath the hand that moulds a shapely urn
    After the potter's foot has stopped its beat,—
From this how history makes itself we learn.

CCXVII

Except the seed fall in th' unconscious earth
Sweet desert rose will never come to birth,
    Except the spirit dwell with mortal clay
Immortal virtues will not show their worth.

CCXVIII

The glory won by Paladin of old,
What matter if by prince or beggar told ! —
    Will draught of water have a different taste
If drinking-cup be made of earth or gold ?

CCXIX

Around the common well of desert town
Worn stones are grooved, ropes running up and down ;
    So have men leveled walls of circumstance,
And so have worn away a life's renown.

CCXX

Where camels pass a hollow track is shown,
Next day the track with sand is overblown,
    And of that sand the very smallest grains
Are dust of princes otherwise unknown.

CCXXI

The rippled sand is scrawled with curves perplexed,
What one day writes is cancelled by the next;
    Let *moullah* scan the scroll with care he finds
Allah il Allah runs the repeated text.

CCXXII

The leader shambling o'er a sandy place
Leaves lines for second camel to erase,-
    Lines of our destiny though writ in dust
No skill of ours availeth to efface.

CCXXIII

The years I journey through this desert land
My shadow goes beside me o'er the sand;
    Not otherwise on all the way of life
Go Self and Soul together hand in hand.

CCXXIV

Ah me! the praisers of my life are few,
How many scorn the work I have to do!
   And yet I find a comfort in the thought,
The Prophet was a camel driver too.

CCXXV

The man who makes his soul a beast to bear
His own vexations with another's care,
   May find before he comes to halting-place
He has of this world claimed too large a share.

CXXVI

Why should the purpose of my patron be
Always to burden both himself and me?
   Himself with care, with toil my weary limbs;—
The Prophet's boast was of his poverty.

CCXXVII

If for his good was man from Eden driven,
If for a blessing toil and sweat were given,
   How has he from the greatness of his soul
For others' good in self-denial striven!

CCXXVIII

Large charities the liberal-minded planned,
Grieved that he could not Fortune's aid command;
    But Money said, "The miser knows my worth,
And so it is I come to miser's hand."

CCXXIX

Time, in his dealings, takes our hopes in trust,
Bright hopes they are which he permits to rust,
    When in the future we demand them back
Then time delivers nought but worthless dust.

CCXXX

Who fills his coffers full of glittering gold
May feast his miser's gaze when he is old,
    But let him look into his miser's heart
And there he finds but emptiness and cold.

CCXXXI

Spendthrift of life in toil and sacrifice,
That he may heap the treasured gold, is wise
    If with his winning he has gained the craft
To gild with this the walls of Paradise.

CCXXXII

Who would engage upon a dangerous quest
Will find that private counsel is the best; —
    When Alexander marched against the East
At night his tent was pitched to front the west.

CCXXXIII

Of every creature Allah wills the fate,
He wills the place of death, He wills the date; —
    Be this the day, be Samarkand the place,
To-day our train will pass that city's gate.

CCXXXIV

We plan for time but Allah plans for aye;
We pray for good but Allah answers "Nay;"
    Not that the good we crave is aught but good,—
A greater good the learning to obey.

CCXXXV

Like camels men are doomed to travel o'er
The waste 'twixt past and future, and explore,
    Leave all the world to those who later come
And follow after those have gone before.

CCXXXVI

As reach of land between opposing seas,
Low reef of shifting sand aye washed by these,
   Man walks this narrow span with confidence,
Its two abutments vast eternities.

CCXXXVII

Time has a past outrunning history,
A future to whose limits none can see,
   And yet with all its measureless extent
Time's but a fragment of eternity.

CCXXXVIII

Age ends its labors as Youth ends its play,
Not long at Life's successive inns we stay;
   We drain our cups before the common fire,
Pay off the score, and then are on our way.

CCXXXIX

We leave Life's entertainment as we came,
All wealth is nought — if rich or poor, the same;
   And those on whom has Fortune smiled the most
Confess its use was winning of the game.

CCXL

If any man by studious thought has come
To comprehend of wisdom all its sum,
  He has not lisped of this one word to us—
In leash of wiser thoughts his lips are dumb.

CCXLI

He is not blind who can the Prophet read,
He is not deaf who gives the beggar heed;
  But he who speaks not in another's woe
Words of compassion — he is dumb indeed.

CCXLII

The path across the desert leads to where
Damascus lies among its gardens fair,—
  Life's path that runs beyond our mortal sight
Will end at last, and we be happy there.

CCXLIII

From happy scenes, from home and kindred banned,
Went Ishmael's mother into desert land,
  In very shame she watched her luckless child,
Nor saw Heaven's angel close beside her stand.

CCXLIV

Somewhere on earth a patient soul doth wait
Long, weary searching of its lonely mate,
　　Be their first meeting on the desert wide,
And right before them opens Eden's gate.

CCXLV

Who travels far abroad through regions vast
Comes back no wiser for his toil at last
　　Than he who in the city's gateway sits
And watches eager pilgrims hurrying past.

CCXLVI

Among the crowd went Obeyd all alone,
To all he met he made his trouble known,
　　And, coming back, reported to his friends
He found each heart had trouble of its own.

CCXLVII

Were I, O Love, a poor despised thing,
Helpless as you would be with broken wing,
　　In my despair you would be at my side,
As Fortune scorned, you would the closer cling!

CCXLVIII

How on my thought will faithful memory wait
Of how we twain went from the city gate,—
　　My love with me far as the parting well,
And how thenceforth my way is desolate !

CCXLIX

I dreamed that Paradise I wandered through,
Its loveliness lay open to my view;
　　Walk, Love, with me this desert track, and then
Will all the promise of that dream come true.

CCL

Day breaks, the east with glory's all ablaze,
For me have broken thus how many days !
　　And yet this dawns as none had dawned before,
Their memory 's lost in wonder as we gaze !

CCLI

Is Spring at hand, the darling of the year ?
Is Spring at hand ? do meadows green appear ?
　　I look abroad, I see not my beloved : —
No, meadows are not green, Spring is not here !

CCLII

The sunset glory on the mountain lies,
Lies on the clouds to which those summits rise ; —
   In hush of evening's solemn hour is held
This golden wedding of the earth and skies !

CCLIII

How sight of home the toil-worn traveler cheers
When after desert march his home appears !
   Heaven after life shall gladden us the more
Eternity transcends our mortal years.

CCLIV

This track that lies across the desert wide
Ends under palm trees on the further side ;—
   Be patient, Soul of mine, the way of life
Will lead to blessings that are here denied.

CCLV

Yea, when the unseen messenger shall call,
When over lights of heaven shall darkness fall,
   Then will Archangel put the scroll away,
And Allah stand revealed — the All-in-all.

CCLVI

One hears the evening waters gently flow,
Another hears the *bulbul's* plaint of woe, —
    To my glad ear the voice of my beloved
Sounds. in that melting music, soft and low.

CCLVII

Is that a star low shining ? — Who can tell ! —
Below the rim of night's cerulean bell?
    The night is cloudy ; — no, 'tis not a star ; —
My love awaits me at the parting well !

CCLVIII

O joy of pilgrim, now his journey 's o'er,
Now that he enters at his low tent door !
    If home and kindred furnish so great joy
What joy supernal Heaven must have in store !

CCLIX

O grace of Allah giving faithful friend
To wait my coming at the journey's end !
    And equal grace Thyself to go with me,
Nor halt however long the way I wend !

Two pilgrims met in mosque at *El Meshed*,
One from the living came, one from the dead :
    The ghost was Obeyd from his desert march,
The mortal — who records what this one said.

THE CAMEL'S THOUGHTS

REBEKAH at the desert fountain's brink
To Abraham's servant gives cool draught to drink, —
     " I'll draw," she says, " for thirsty camel, too,"
What must the wayworn, thirsty camel think!

THE CAMEL'S THOUGHTS

I

ONE after one the camels start away
From smouldering camp-fires in the morning gray,
   One after one the loitering line comes in
To evening camp-fires at the close of day.

II

Let but one camel pass and you have there
Signs of his passing, seen at spaces rare ;
   But let the train come after in his lead
And soon the track is made a thoroughfare.

III

Slow o'er the desert winds the camel train,
Across the heavens drift heavy clouds of rain,
   These yield their charge when mountains stay their
      course,
Poor camels theirs when cities proud they gain.

IV

As ship becalmed is seen all day to stand
No farther off, no nearer to the land,
   So camels seem to keep the selfsame spot
Upon this smooth monotony of sand.

V

The track in burning sand before me lies, ·
Far on the low horizon palms arise,
   Fast as I haste to gain the halting place
The vision of the palms before me flies.

VI

Before the blast white wave at Bushine curls,
Wild storm of sand across the desert whirls,
   Through blinding storm my lonely way I go
As through the waves lone diver goes for pearls.

VII

Unnumbered dangers haunt the desert wide,
By lonely trails doth violence abide,
   And there I find my driver follows close
As timid child clings to its mother's side.

VIII

With man on desert track I take the lead,
He follows, urging me to greater speed,
    Not knowing that with hunger and with thirst
We both are driven along by direst need.

IX

Enough to me each day its grief and bale,
Enough that in my task I do not fail ;
    My driver borrows from the days to come,
Thinks how his deeds shall sound in future tale.

X

My master takes good care his slave be fed
If only for some service coveted,
    Will not then He who owns both lord and slave
Provide for slave and lord their daily bread ?

XI

Two things to simple-minded man are known, —
That husbandman must reap what he hath sown,
    That cub of wolf reared in the homes of men
Becomes no less a wolf when it is grown.

XII

Men need a higher wisdom yet to gain,
Or else content with us, poor beasts, remain ;
   Know good from evil or else nothing know,
For all between is misery and pain.

XIII

How have I seen in Georgian Tiflis
Men hail their conquering chief till daylight cease !
   Seen then the chief turn sorrowful away, —
The praise of courtiers brings so little peace.

XIV

For fame of leader camels care the least,
To what he leads concerns both man and beast ;—
   Who takes the vulture for a desert guide
Full soon will come to most unsavory feast.

XV

Rich fabrics made in shops of Teheran
Must go, for sale, to mart of Ispahan ;
   And goods from thence be taken in return
To suit the whim of fickle-minded man.

XVI

Through burning sands and over slippery stones
We make our toilsome way with sighs and groans;
   To sate men's greed must camels spend their lives,
To mark the road for him leave whitening bones.

XVII

A comrade little fit for us is Fear
While on our lonely way we travel here,
   But when we find Fear pressing to our side
We note that pain and anguish disappear.

XVIII

Blest that *mirage* whose magic charm can cheat
With show of water dreadful Syrian heat,
   That leads with hope the faltering camel train
O'er cruel sands that scorch the camels' feet.

XIX

On desert route 'tis not the beast of prey
My master fears the most by night, by day ;
   ' Tis not the lion crouching in the path,
But murderous robber ambushed by the way.

XX

Men sit with folded hands, they wait and pray
That Fortune, still indulgent, turn their way;
   When hungry camel famishes for food
He stretches out his neck to reach the hay.

XXI

All creatures have their nature, each its own,
The camel in the desert feeds alone;
   The dog, invited to a princely feast,
Will, underneath the table, gnaw a bone.

XXII

The wild gazelle, content with scanty fare,
Feeds over burning sand of desert bare;
   'Tis not so much she loves th' unfruitful waste
As that the foot of man comes seldom there.

XXIII

When he the failings of another sees,
My driver ready is to carp at these;
   Slow plodding on the desert's sandy road,
I meditate my own infirmities.

XXIV

Here toil and need and misery are rife,
And heat and dust and bitterness of strife;
　　At last a bed upon the yielding sand,
And this, it seems to me, is all of life.

XXV

I wonder why men cross the desert wide
And then recross unto the former side;
　　What was the sandy waste created for
Except the tribes and nations to divide?

XXVI

The starveling shrub half buried in the sand,
By feverish blast of hot sirocco fanned,
　　Gives from its dried and crumpled leaves the breath
Of bitterness felt by its native land.

XXVII

No finger-post is needed for a guide
To pilgrims who across the desert ride,
　　From end to end the dismal way is marked
With bleaching bones of camels that have died.

XXVIII

Is it that any power above can be
Such to my master as he is to me,
    Some sovereign ruling mankind absolute
Yet failing to avert man's destiny ?

XXIX

We luckless camels kneel upon the road
When we take up or when we leave our load :
    My driver bows him prostrate in the dust, —
If nevermore to rise, the better mode.

XXX

Should drop of rain fall in the desert here
'T would instantly as vapor disappear,
    The happy drop that falls on marigold
Is folded to the heart as treasure dear.

XXXI

The wind at midnight cold as winter blew,
The sunrise brings the summer's heat anew,
    In Kashmir's vale the rose blooms all the year,
The orange never bids the spring adieu.

XXXII

In winter time by Allah's thoughtful care
With greater cold grows thicker camel's hair,
    My driver has to guard against the frost
And purchase him a robe at Persian fair.

XXXIII

Poor silly grouse knows what a simple thing
It is in desert drought to find a spring,
    My master would not know which way to fly
Were gracious Heaven to give him ample wing.

XXXIV

Where height of dangerous pass is to be won
Most praise is his who has the way begun,
    For he has not alone to climb the way,
He also has to show it can be done.

XXXV

In camp our driver calls, "What of the night?
Is it far spent, dawns now the eastern light?"
    "Yea, starry watchers leave celestial post
As glorious day's outriders come in sight!"

XXXVI

Of storm and somber shadows men complain,
With hope look for bright sunshine once again;
   My driver, sleeping in his desert tent,
Has dream no sweeter than of falling rain.

XXXVII

On burning sand spread under burning sky
From well to well do trails of traffic lie,—
   What cares the merchant that here Thirst abides
And watches famished caravans go by?

XXXVIII

Across the sand long lines of camels wind,
No shade, no water and no food they find;
   How well is desert guarded against Life,
To Death alone hospitable and kind.

XXXIX

What have I in my toilsome life where all
Is daily drudgery whate'er befall?
   What pleasure, looking backward on the road?—
To care for what's to come is only thrall.

XL

In fragrance sweet the withering flower gives
What from its life the desert shrub receives;
   'Tis only after death that can be known
What in me or my driver chiefly lives.

XLI

By camel's foot or hoof of horse is traced
A crescent moon upon the desert waste,
   Let lengthened train come slowly shambling by
And soon all sign of crescent is effaced.

XLII

This weary waste of sand that shimmers so
As floor of furnace under fiery glow,
   Pales in the moonlight, and I walk it then
As plodding over fields of drifted snow.

XLIII

The robber rain that carries sands away
Collects in stagnant pools deep beds of clay,
   The solvent water binds the desert dust
In sun-dried walls defensive of Cathay.

XLIV

That gold whose gleam makes glad the miser's eyes
Upon the camel's back a burden lies,
  Makes wearisome long journey of the day
Than load of quarried stone no otherwise.

XLV

My journey leads me through a songless land,
Not e'en the cricket's chirp on either hand;
  Nor is the silence of the desert broke
By camel's muffled footfall on the sand.

XLVI

In haunts of men do swallows make their home,
They, twittering, fly round minaret and dome;
  In comradeship with pestilence and death,
Grim, silent vultures o'er the desert roam.

XLVII

My driver in his human wisdom knows
That from life's labors death will bring repose,
  And yet, with knowledge of both life and death,
He comes through life complaining to its close.

XLVIII

The meanest dog, left to himself to go
By fancy led and coursing fast or slow,
 Has better fortune than the lion has
That paces gilded prison to and fro.

XLIX

To camel's thoughts how many a curious thing
The desert and the market-place will bring !
 Who serves one master only — he 's a slave ;
Who is the slave of millions — he 's a king.

L

On either side our path an ambuscade
By hostile bands of circumstance is laid,
 With fewer risks the desert course is run
As with the greater speed the course is made.

LI

Stars disappear soon as the day comes on,
Invisible in brightness of the dawn,
 Fixed at their post, but who can point the way
By which the vanished morning frost is gone ?

LII

Hot blows the wind from out the torrid south,
Hot as the blast comes from the furnace mouth,
    Yet grateful to the land to which it goes
As mists from chilly north to desert drouth.

LIII

Far on the weary road my driver sees
Stand out against the sky tall clump of trees,
    Rejoicing at their sight for well he knows
Cool springs of water overhung by these.

LIV

Long march is over, bells their tinkling cease,
From heavy burden camel has release,
    My driver, too, so many dangers run,
With friends at last enjoys a grateful peace.

O WELCOME rest to travel-worn and sore !

O welcome sleeping when the march is o'er !

   Is it that life leads ever on to death,

Is death a resting from life evermore ?

FROM THE DESERT

WELL OF PARTING

NOT in the city gate,
    ' Mid mad confusion of the crowded street,
Where eager sellers wait
    For eager buyers 'mong the throng they meet,
Are words of farewell said by man to man
At ancient Ispahan.

With him who goes abroad
    Through Persia's worn-out, empty, lonesome land,
Upon the desert road
    His friend goes, too. until at length they stand
Beneath the tree where, through long ages dead,
Have farewell words been said.

There by the wayside well
    Dug by their ancestors in thirsty plain,
Whose stones worn deeply tell
    Of ropes let down, of ropes drawn up again,
They part, the one on desert paths to roam
The other going home.

Ah, who shall know the end
    Awaiting either in the coming years
When friend goes with his friend
    To well of parting, sad good-bye, and tears !
One forward goes a lone wayfaring man,
One back to Ispahan.

EL TEKBIR

" Do ye year the voice of angel or of mortal
 Chant the praises of the Prophet far or near ;
From the desert round about us or Heaven's portal,
 Falleth any sound of worship on the ear ? "
Thus the Khalif questioned closely his attendants
 In the still and lonely watches of the night,
While the crescent of their faith with its resplendence
 Rendered all the desert landscape ghostly white.

" Not a whisper low from angel lips or mortal
 In the stillness of the desert do we hear,
Not a strain of song escaping from Heaven's portal
 Cometh to the eager soul or listening ear."
Thus the soldiers spake the Khalif : — by this token
 Well their chieftain knew he heard the low *Tekbir*,
This it was of which his heavenly guest had spoken,
 Sounding only to his hearing soft and clear.

Glad the Khalif, — in his light unquiet sleeping,
 In the deeply silent watches of the night,
To his tent past guards their lonely vigil keeping
 All unseen had come a messenger of light ;

By the bedside of the Khalif stood the stranger,
　　Bade the troubled sleeper be of hearty cheer,
For a voice should lead his people out of danger,—
　　Voice that only Allah's chosen one could hear.

"Follow," said the stranger, "where that voice shall call
　　　　thee
　　Though it lead thee through the desert wild and drear,
In obedience no evil can befall thee,
　　Let thy people also follow without fear:
Where it stayeth thou shalt found for them a city,
　　War and pestilence shall nevermore come near;
Rise and lead thy trusting followers in pity,
　　Rise and listen for the mystical *Tekbir!*"

At the dawn the Khalif forward boldly riding
　　Bore the standard of the Prophet in the van,
Followed close upon his low mysterious guiding,
　　Careless aught of earth or sky above to scan;
When at eve that mystic chant no longer sounded
　　There the tired legion halted, horse and man,
There the *Kibleh* of the Prophet's faith was founded,
　　There was traced the holy city of Kairwan.

SID BEL ABBAS

SID BEL ABBAS good and wise,—
Rest his soul in Paradise—
Holy, while yet in the flesh,
 In the guiltless life he led,
Coming once to Marakesh
 Begged to beg his daily bread.

Sainted beggars in the gate
Heard his plea disconsolate,
Poor and scanty their supplies
 When their needs were at the least,
How could daily alms suffice
 If their numbers were increased?

For reply was sent to him
Bowl with water to the brim,
This was meant to indicate
 Room was none for him to try,
Seated in the city gate,
 Alms to ask of passers-by.

Can the bowl receive aught more
And the waters not run o'er?
" Will he join the holy men
 At the gate and in the tent,
Let the bowl return again
 Holding more than they have sent."

Sid bel Abbas then replies,—
Rest his soul in Paradise—
Plucks a drooping desert rose,
 Lets it drink till it is whole,
Fresh the fragrant flower goes
 With the water in the bowl.

KOSHAIRA

FROM its rock-encircled fountain
 Runs the river clear and cold,
Down the slope of Syrian mountain,
 Over sands of shining gold;
Bright the current of Koshaira,
 Dark its mystery of old
Linked with Kadi of Palmyra,
 By Arabian poet told.

True the story, or invented,
 Be it fact, or Fancy's dream,
Once the Khalif Mamoun tented
 By the margin of the stream;
Musing on his present duty,
 Idly watching sportive bream,
Of a more than common beauty
 Did the fish to Mamoun seem.

Summoning a trusty waiter,
    Promised he a rich reward
If that bream were served him later
    Smoking hot on evening board.
Willingly the slave was hired;
    From the shallows of the ford
Soon he brought the fish admired,
    Pleased he showed it to his lord.

While the Khalif idly lingers,
    Lost in wonderment complete,
Slips the fish through idle fingers,
    To his fellows makes retreat;
In the shallow water plashes
    Where the shore and river meet,
Chilly cold the bath he dashes
    On the Arab's sandalled feet.

And the touch of that cold river
    Gives Mamoun a sudden start,
Sends an evil-boding shiver
    Through the chambers of his heart

He recalls the warning spoken
    With the shrewd diviner's art,
He recalls the promised token
    To foreshow the fatal dart.

Then did Mamoun, cold and weary,
    By the gloom of Fate oppressed,
For the river's name make query
    Though its mystic sense he guessed;—
Came reply in soothing numbers
    To his spirit sore distressed,
For " Koshaira" bids to slumbers,—
    " Stretch thy feet out here and rest."

BELFRY OF ALEPPO

UNDERNEATH the sky of Syria unclouded,
　　Studded with the constellations burning bright,
Lies the Bedouin, in his *burnous* closely shrouded,
　　On a waste of sandy desert gleaming white;
Round about the child of Ishmael soundly sleeping
　　All the hungry packs of desert creatures prowl,
With a light and stealthy footstep softly creeping,
　　Answering back the startled cry with surly growl.

Not at all the sleeper heeds the angry growling,
　　So familiar is that discord to his ear—
Yell of tiger and the hungry jackal's howling,
　　Cries of rage and terror, uttered far and near;
But at midnight he is wakened from his slumbers
　　By a human cry borne on the desert air;
The muezzin's call in slow, harmonious numbers,
　　Seems to summon true believers unto prayer.

"Pity, Allah, pity us!" the voice is crying;
　"Have compassion on our weakness in Thy might;
Show us pity, Lord, who art Thyself undying,
　Us who daily fall and perish in Thy sight!"
Strange the cry itself, and no less strange the hour,
　Nowhere else was ever midnight summons heard,—
'Tis the ancient calling from Aleppo's tower,
　From the days of Omar cried in Grecian word.

When the Moslem under Khaled fierce assailing
　Drove the Christians from their altars and their homes,
Then the Prophet's faith and worship, all prevailing,
　Changed to Sunnee mosques their consecrated domes.
Blotted out the pictures on the wall and ceiling,
　Broke the figures from the mortar and the stone,
From the belfry, for the chime's accordant pealing,
　Sent the loud muezzin's call in plaintive tone.

Thus did fare the church of holy Zacharias
　When Aleppo fell into the Moslem's care.
Then the old, fanatic Khaled, sternly pious,
　Sent aloft to call the faithful unto prayer;

And a servant quick responding to his token,
  Climbed the staircase till its upper stage was found,
But before his lips the holy name had spoken,
  Strangely had he fallen headlong to the ground.

Quick the order was repeated by the master,
  Prompt a follower responded to the call,
Up the dizzy staircase mounting fast and faster,
  He was all the sooner coming to his fall.
Then the captain for the third time gave his order,
  Bade a trusty guardsman to the belfry go,
In obedience turned away the veteran warder, —
  First he knelt in prayer within the church below.

While the pious Moslem proffered his petition,
  Praying to escape the death his comrades died,
Came the holy Zacharias, says tradition,
  Stood and listened with compassion at his side.
Then the vision bade the warder to the tower,
  Promised safety for one act of faith alone;
Let muezzins evermore at midnight hour
  For this sacrilege the litany intone.

Thus it is that through each lengthening generation
  Handed down has been the ancient Christian prayer;
Thus it is that at Aleppo's lonely station
  Still muezzins mount each night the belfry stair.
" Pity, Allah, pity ! " still the voice is crying,
  " Have compassion on our weakness in Thy might;
Show us pity, Lord, who art Thyself undying,
  Us who daily fall and perish in Thy sight ! "

THE DESERT STREAM

BORN of the winter's snow
    Over Syrian mountain spread,
In the heat of the summer's glow
    When the sun burns overhead ;
On the mountain's shoulder high,
In the blue fields of the sky
    When the moon hangs low
    And the staid stars go
Their unheralded marches by.

Feeling the pulses strong
    Of a new and unworn life,
How the torrent rushes along
    In the maddened frenzy of strife !
Impatient the waters stay,
Gladly they hurry away,
    And merry their song
    As they hasten along
Whether by night or by day.

Leaping adown the rocks,
 Over broken masses of ledge,
Baffled by frequent shocks
 Do they come to the cataract's edge ;
Headlong plunging they go
Into the basin below
 Where the glassy pool,
 Fern-shaded and cool,
Sleeps on in the noontide glow.

Hither the lioness leads
 Through the tangled border of wood,
Crawling among the reeds,
 Her thirsty and famishing brood ;
Daintily setting her paw,
Greedily licking her jaw,
 Now she laps the flood
 As she lapped the blood
Of the slain kid, reeking and raw.

With a low and angry growl
    She answers the leopard's cry,
The yell, the snarl, and the howl
    Of the tigress prowling nigh ;
From the desert these come to the brink
Of the mountain river to drink ;
    Having lapped their fill.
    All surly and still
Back to the jungle they slink.

Even the palm trees tall,
    Oleanders fair as a dream
Owe their loveliness all
    To the generous-hearted Stream ;
Crowding close to its side
Reeds and rushes abide,
    And they drink their fill
    Of the waters so still
That under their shadow hide.

By the scorching breezes fanned
    From the desert's feverish breath,
Drunk by the hissing sand
    In the hideous valley of death;
From its oozy channel strayed
The seething current is stayed,
    And 'tis lost at last
    In the desert so vast
'Neath the withering myrtle's shade.

ZULEÏKA

INTO exile from thee am I driven, Zuleïka,
  Zuleïka, my pearl, my rich treasure;
I am driven to the desert to die, Zuleïka,
  Zuleïka, my pearl, my rich treasure;
To gazelles all my trouble I've told, Zuleïka,
  Zuleïka, my pearl, my rich treasure;
The gazelles have my trouble but mocked, Zuleïka,
  Zuleïka, my pearl, my rich treasure.

*   *   *   *   *   *   *

In mirage I behold thee again, Zuleïka,
  Zuleïka, my peri from heaven;
But, alas! from me flies the mirage, Zuleïka,
  Zuleïka, my peri from heaven.
With a thirst that's consuming I burn, Zuleïka,
  Zuleïka, my peri from heaven;
No, the thirst for thy kisses it is, Zuleïka,
  Zuleïka, my peri from heaven.
I drink and I live;—lo, a garden of pleasures!
  Zuleïka, my peri from heaven;
'Tis paradise! gladly for thee do I perish,
  Zuleïka, my peri from heaven!

THE PHANTOM TRAIN

IN peace was pitched the pilgrim tent
    Upon the desert sand,
Beside the track where pilgrims went
    To Mecca's holy land ;
And in the fading of the day,
    The coming of the night,
At peace poor weary pilgrims lay
    In Allah's watchful sight.

But one, the patriarch of them all,
    As Abraham of yore,
Sat, watching folds of darkness fall,
    Beside the low tent door ;
And, as along the dusky road
    He strained his feeble sight,
From out the gloom a figure strode
    Close shrouded all in white.

It was the leader of a train,
    As of a pilgrim band,
Slow winding over desert plain
    Towards the holy land;
A train of camels laden sore
    Came through the misty night,
The burdens on their backs they bore
    With funeral palls were dight.

No sound of footfall on the sand,
    Of tinkling bell no sound,
The old man watched the coming band
    In mystery profound;
He rose to greet it drawing near —
    It loomed against the sky —
" Peace!" spake the old man without fear,
    And " Peace!" the calm reply.

"As Allah willed, the daylight went,
    The day will come again,
Rest thou this night within my tent,
    And rest thy weary train;

His love will pious pilgrims keep
    Long as life's road they fare,
And when at last they fall asleep
    They sleep in Allah's care."

" Nay, urge me not," the leader said,
    ' Tis time my train should go,
' Tis theirs to bear the Moslem dead
    O'er deserts to and fro ;
The faithful who abroad have died
    May rest in holy place,
To faithless Meccans is denied
    This share in Allah's grace.

" On earth it seems to mortal eyes
    That night must follow day,
But to the realms of Paradise
    The world is light for aye ;
We travel in that selfsame light
    Along a lighted way,
And spirits waiting wished-for sight
    Forbid that we should stay.

" This time we bring from distant Spain
    Heroic ones who fell
Fierce fighting on Grenada's plain
    Against the infidel ;
And of that number there is one —
    A young, a beauteous boy —
The mother waits her darling son,
    We stay that mother's joy."

The old man asks the glorious name,
    And then entreaties cease ;
He bids the leader, as he came,
    " With Allah go in peace ! "
The name that falls upon his ears
    Is a familiar one,
Kept sacred through life's closing years —
    That of his youngest son.